We ♡ Our School!

A Read-Together Rebus Story

by Judy Sierra

pictures by Linda Davick

Alfred A. Knopf New York

"It's the first day of school,"

Said the in the pool.

"I must put on my  and my coat."

With 2 books in his pack

That he wore on his back,

He sailed off to school in a .

S. S. RIBBET

The smart little

Rode to school in a .

"Wait for me!" cried the polka-dot .

A , who was late,

Made a STOP by the gate,

And the hitched a ride on her tail.

The teacher, Tom Burkey,

A very nice ,

Waited for them at the .

They all wrote their names,

They played ABC games,

And built towers of on the floor.

ABCDEFGHIJKLMNOPQRSTUVWXY
Snail
FROG
MOUSE
DUCK
FROG

Mrs. taught art

From a big cart.

The helped the draw a .

"Oh, no!" quacked the .

"My are stuck."

"I'll fix them for you," squeaked the .

The polka-dot snail

Brought her lunch in a 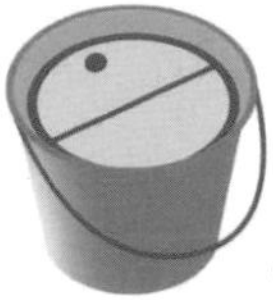 .

The duck had some soup in a  .

The frog caught a  ,

And the mouse shared her

With their teacher, who gobbled it  .

They counted to 10,

And back  again,

While their teacher took out his .

They sang about sharing,

And helping, and caring,

And everyone felt like a  .

1
2
3
4
5
6
7
8
9
10

Then they climbed in the

With the smart little duck.

The frog put his on the back.

And they rode to the pool,

Shouting, "We our school!

RIBBET! SQUEAK! BLOOP, BLOOP! QUACK! QUACK!"

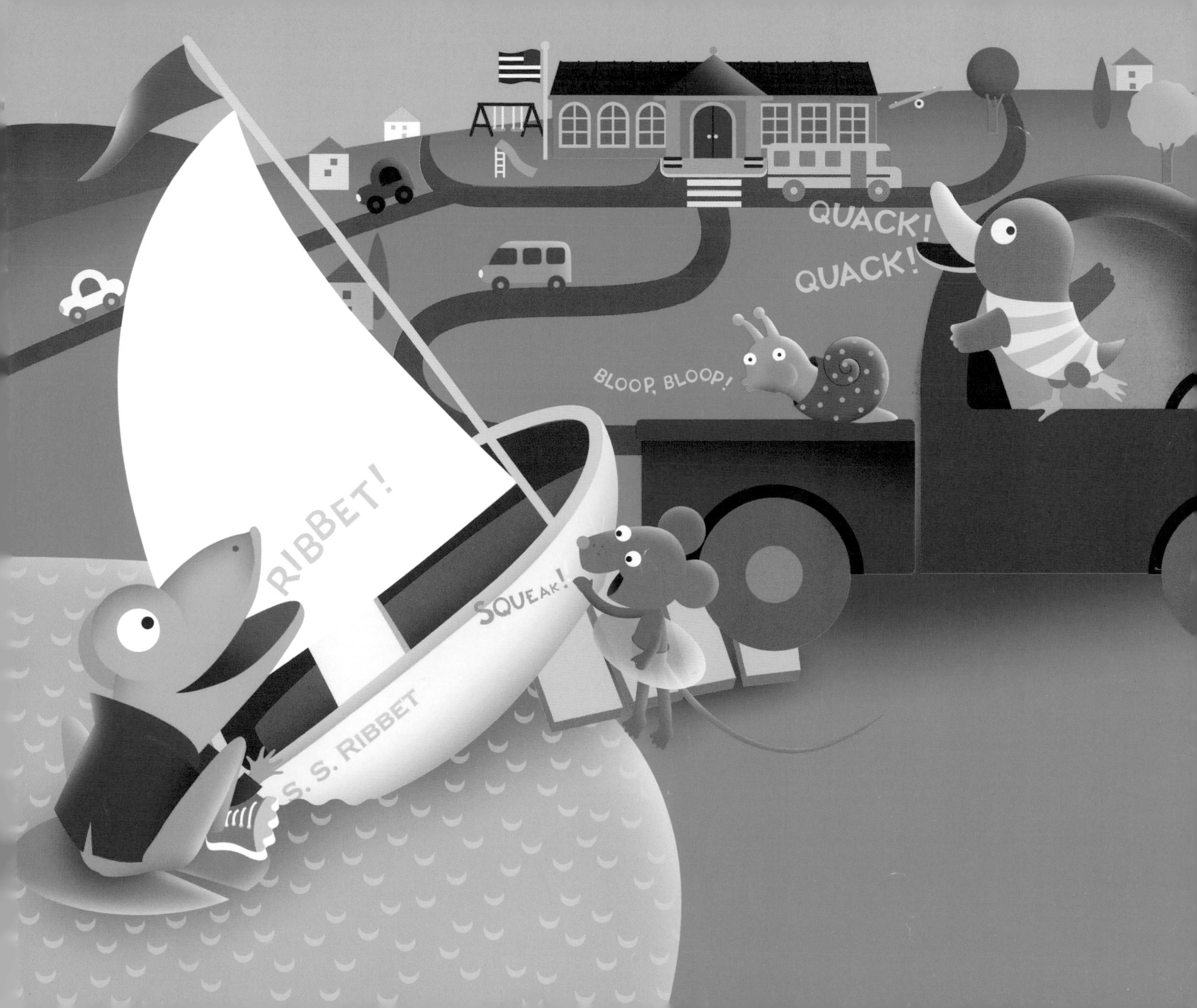
QUACK!
QUACK!
BLOOP, BLOOP!
RIBBET!
SQUEAK!
S. S. RIBBET

THIS IS A BORZOI BOOK PUBLISHED BY ALFRED A. KNOPF

Visit us on the Web! www.randomhouse.com/kids

Educators and librarians, for a variety of teaching tools, visit us at www.randomhouse.com/teachers

Library of Congress Cataloging-in-Publication Data
Sierra, Judy.
We love our school! / by Judy Sierra ; illustrated by Linda Davick. — 1st ed.
p. cm.
Summary: Rhyming text with rebuses follows a group of animals through their first day of school.
ISBN 978-0-375-86728-6 (trade) — ISBN 978-0-375-96728-3 (lib. bdg.)
[1. Stories in rhyme. 2. First day of school—Fiction. 3. Schools—Fiction. 4. Animals—Fiction. 5. Rebuses.]
I. Davick, Linda, ill. II. Title.
PZ8.3.S577We 2011
[E]—dc22 2009039581

MANUFACTURED IN MALAYSIA
June 2011
10 9 8 7 6 5 4 3 2 1

First Edition

To Jacob

—J.S.

To Edmond Inomoto

—L.D.